Close Your Eyes

by Robyn Wilson-Owen

Boxer Books

It's time for bed.

It's time to close your eyes.

What do you see if
you close them tight?

Do you see colors,
bright and light?

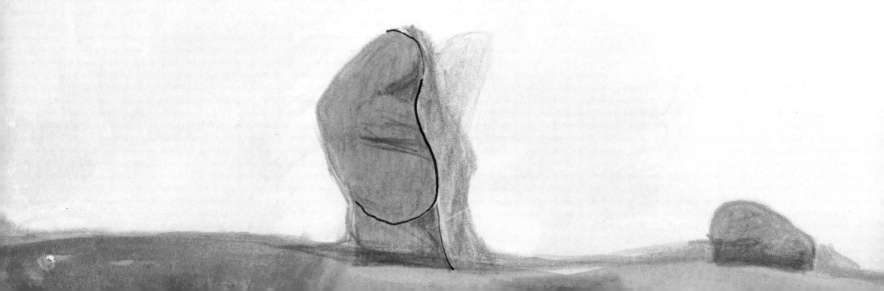

Where will you go? What will you see?

It's time for an adventure.

Who will you be?

Peep through a half-open eye.
Is the world in black and white?

Not a single color,
just shades of the night.

Open them. Close them.
Open them. Close them.

Do you see pictures flickering by?

Maybe a bear? Stars in the sky?

If I stroke
your nose
softly, do
your eyes
feel heavy?

Can you feel them closing?
I think we're almost ready.

You're
sinking
into bed.
Calm and
quiet and
warm.
Softly,
slowly,
safe from
any storm.

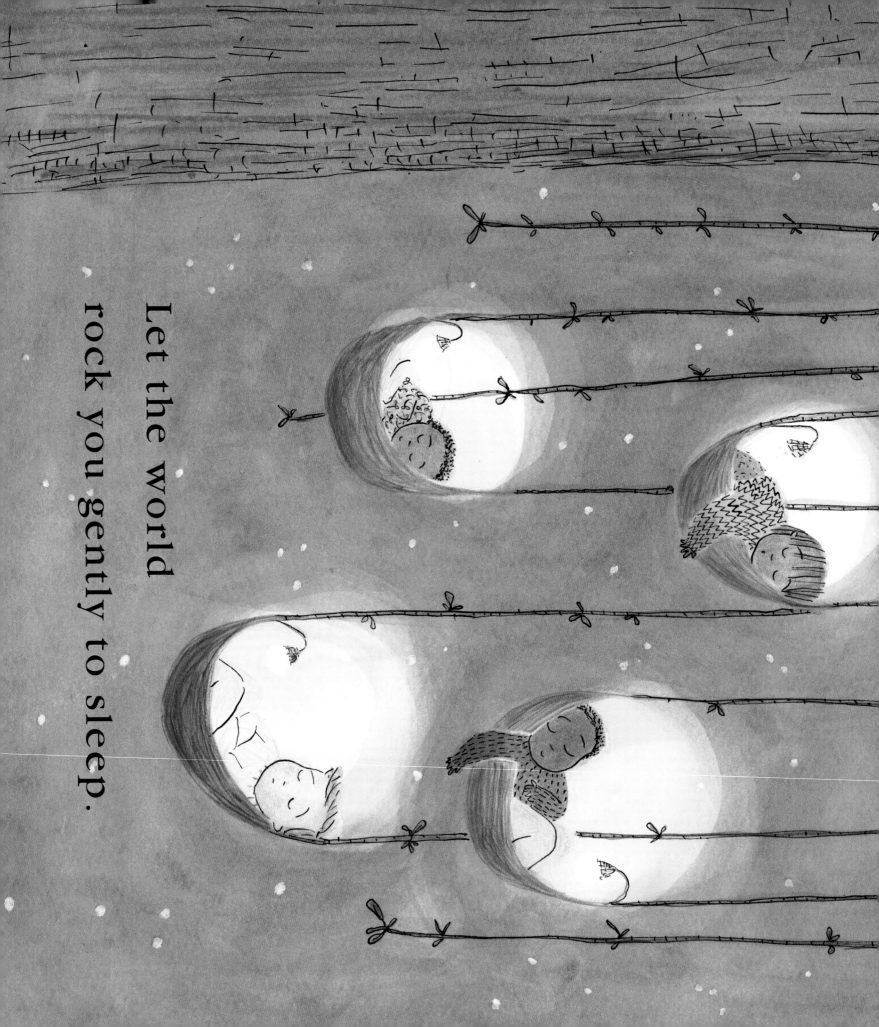

Let the world
rock you gently to sleep.

Can you keep
your eyes
closed? Listen
and don't peek.

Keep your eyes closed,
what do you see?

The day that's just ended,
or one yet to be?

Are you the star
in your story?
Leading your
friends on ahead...

Can you drift back home
through the night-time?

Back to your cozy, warm bed.

For Martha, Greta, and Ida.

Robyn Wilson-Owen

First published in North America in 2021 by Boxer Books Limited.
www.boxerbooks.com
Boxer® is a registered trademark of Boxer Books Limited.